STEP INTO READING®

STEP 3

MARC BROWN

ARTHUR'S READING TRICK

Random House 🏠 New York

Step into Reading, Random House, and the Random House colophon are registered trademarks of Random House, Inc.

Arthur is a registered trademark of Marc Brown.

Grateful acknowledgment is made to Dr. Seuss Enterprises, L.P. for permission to reprint a depiction and the title of *Green Eggs and Ham* by Dr. Seuss, ™ and © Dr. Seuss Enterprises, L.P. 1960. All Rights Reserved.

Visit us on the Web! www.stepintoreading.com

Educators and librarians, for a variety of teaching tools, visit us at www.randomhouse.com/teachers

Library of Congress Cataloging-in-Publication Data
Brown, Marc Tolon.
Arthur's reading trick / Marc Brown. — 1st ed.
p. cm. — (Step into reading. Step 3 reader)
Summary: Arthur's sister D.W. tries to use a reading trick to get Arthur to change Baby Kate's diapers.
ISBN 978-0-375-82977-2 (trade pbk.) — ISBN 978-0-375-92977-9 (lib. bdg.)
[1. Reading—Fiction. 2. Brothers and sisters—Fiction. 3. Babies—Fiction. 4. Aardvark—Fiction.] I. Title.
PZ7.B81618Arqb 2009
[E]—dc22 2008050979

Printed in the United States of America 10 9 8 7 6 5 4 3 2

D.W. could say her ABCs.

She could write them too.

And she could read one book,

Green Eggs and Ham.

She liked to read it to Arthur.

"Oh, no," said Arthur.

"Not again!"

"I bet I can teach Baby Kate
   to read," said D.W.
"I bet you can't," said Arthur.
"And the loser has to change
   Kate's stinky diaper."
"It's a deal," said D.W.

"Work on it," said Arthur,
"while I do my homework."

D.W. got her crayons
and some paper.

She got Kate's red ball
with stars.

She got Kate's little blue car.

And she got Kate's bottle.

D.W. wrote the letters B-A-L-L
on the paper.
Then she held up the red ball
and pointed to the letters.
"What does this say, Kate?"
asked D.W.
"Ball!" said Kate.

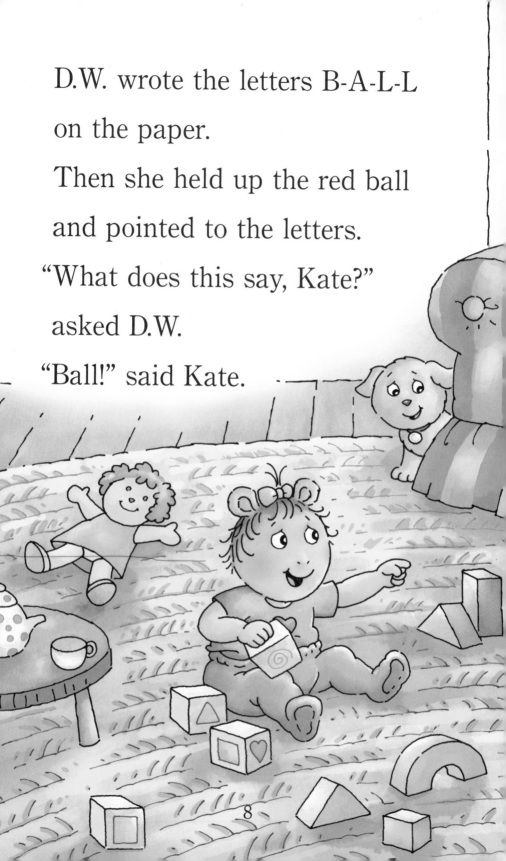

Next D.W. wrote C-A-R.

She held up the blue car.

"What do these letters say?"

D.W. asked Kate.

"Car!" said Kate.

D.W. did the same thing
with Kate's bottle.
And Kate said, "Bottle!"
"Mom, come here," shouted D.W.
"Kate can read!"

"Watch this, Mom," said D.W.
She held up
the ball and the paper
with the letters B-A-L-L.
Kate said, "Ball!"

D.W. did the same thing
with the car and the bottle.
Kate said, "Car!" and "Bottle!"
"See, Mom," said D.W.
"I taught Kate how to read."

Mom smiled and shook her head.

"No, D.W.," said Mom.

"Kate is just saying words

she knows

when she sees those objects.

In two years

you can try teaching her."

Mom went back to her computer.

D.W. thought about changing

stinky diapers.

Then she had an idea.

D.W. put the ball and the car
in her pockets.
She hid the bottle
under the sofa.
"Arthur," she called
up the stairs.
"I taught Kate to read."

"This I have to see,"
said Arthur.

"Hold this paper
in front of Kate,"
D.W. told Arthur.

"Now point to the letters."
D.W. stood behind Arthur.
She held up the ball.

"Ball!" said Kate.

Then D.W. gave him
the paper with the letters C-A-R.
Arthur held it up.
D.W. stood behind Arthur
and waved the car at Kate.
"Car!" said Kate.
"I won the bet," said D.W.
"It's stinky diapers for you!"

CAR

BALL

19

"Not so fast, D.W.," said Arthur.
"Let's try another word."
"Okay, I don't mind," said D.W.
She handed him the paper
with the letters B-O-T-T-L-E.

But Kate's bottle had rolled

way under the sofa.

"Wait a minute," said D.W.

"I'm not ready."

Then Arthur knew D.W.'s trick.

But he had a trick of his own.

He picked up a diaper

from a box of clean diapers.

He held up the paper

with the letters B-O-T-T-L-E.

"What do the letters say, Kate?"

He waved the diaper.

"Diaper!" said Kate.

BOTTLE

DIAPERS

ELIZA

BALL

"I win," said Arthur.

"And it smells like

   Kate needs a clean one, D.W."

"Oh, no!" cried D.W.